D0367758

QUICK!
REVOLTING RASCALS,
SIGN HERE so everyone
knows **this book** belongs
TO YOU.

Madeleine Kem

ROALD DAHL was a spy, ace fighter pilot, chocolate historian and medical inventor. He was also the author of *Charlie and the Chocolate Factory*, *Matilda*, *The BFG* and many more brilliant stories. He remains **THE WORLD'S NUMBER ONE STORYTELLER.**

QUENTIN BLAKE has illustrated more than three hundred books and was Roald Dahl's favourite illustrator. In 1980 he won the prestigious Kate Greenaway Medal. In 1999 he became the first ever Children's Laureate and in 2013 he was knighted for services to illustration.

INTRODUCING . . .

**Little Red
Riding Hood**

Cinderella

Jack

Snow-White

Goldilocks

Wolf

**The Three
Little Pigs**

Books by Roald Dahl

THE BFG
BOY: TALES OF CHILDHOOD
BOY and GOING SOLO
CHARLIE AND THE CHOCOLATE FACTORY
CHARLIE AND THE GREAT GLASS ELEVATOR
THE COMPLETE ADVENTURES OF CHARLIE AND MR WILLY WONKA
DANNY THE CHAMPION OF THE WORLD
THE ENORMOUS CROCODILE
ESIO TROT
FANTASTIC MR FOX
GEORGE'S MARVELLOUS MEDICINE
THE GIRAFFE AND THE PELLY AND ME
GOING SOLO
JAMES AND THE GIANT PEACH
MATILDA
THE MAGIC FINGER
THE TWITS
THE WITCHES

Picture books

DIRTY BEASTS
THE ENORMOUS CROCODILE
THE GIRAFFE AND THE PELLY AND ME
THE MINPINS
REVOLTING RHYMES

Plays

THE BFG: PLAYS FOR CHILDREN (*Adapted by David Wood*)
CHARLIE AND THE CHOCOLATE FACTORY: A PLAY (*Adapted by Richard George*)
DANNY THE CHAMPION OF THE WORLD: PLAYS FOR CHILDREN
(*Adapted by David Wood*)
FANTASTIC MR FOX: A PLAY (*Adapted by Sally Reid*)
JAMES AND THE GIANT PEACH: A PLAY (*Adapted by Richard George*)
THE TWITS: PLAYS FOR CHILDREN (*Adapted by David Wood*)
THE WITCHES: PLAYS FOR CHILDREN (*Adapted by David Wood*)

Teenage fiction

THE GREAT AUTOMATIC GRAMMATIZATOR AND OTHER STORIES
RHYME STEW
SKIN AND OTHER STORIES
THE VICAR OF NIBBLESWICKE
THE WONDERFUL STORY OF HENRY SUGAR AND SIX MORE

Collections

THE ROALD DAHL TREASURY
SONGS AND VERSE

ROALD DAHL

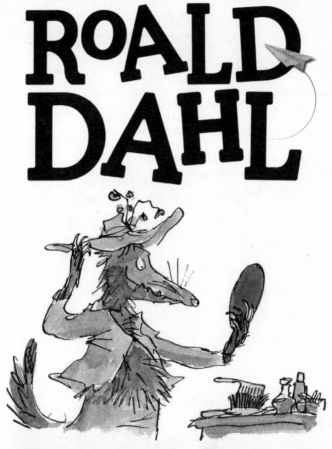

REVOLTING RHYMES

Illustrated by **Quentin Blake**

PUFFIN

PUFFIN BOOKS

UK | USA | Canada | Ireland | Australia
India | New Zealand | South Africa

Puffin Books is part of the Penguin Random House group of companies
whose addresses can be found at global.penguinrandomhouse.com.

www.penguin.co.uk
www.puffin.co.uk
www.ladybird.co.uk

Penguin
Random House
UK

First published by Jonathan Cape 1982
Black-and-white edition published 2012
This edition published by Puffin Books 2016

001

Text copyright © Roald Dahl Nominee Limited, 1982
Illustrations copyright © Quentin Blake, 1982

The moral right of the author and illustrator has been asserted

Typeset in Baskerville MT Std
Printed in Great Britain by Clays Ltd, St Ives plc

A CIP catalogue record for this book is available from the British Library

ISBN: 978-0-141-37412-3

All correspondence to:
Puffin Books
Penguin Random House Children's
80 Strand, London WC2R ORL

MIX
Paper from
responsible sources
FSC
www.fsc.org   FSC® C018179

Penguin Random House is committed to a
sustainable future for our business, our readers
and our planet. This book is made from Forest
Stewardship Council® certified paper.

CONTENTS

Cinderella   1

Jack and the Beanstalk   11

Snow-White and the Seven Dwarfs   21

Goldilocks and the Three Bears   31

Little Red Riding Hood and the Wolf   41

The Three Little Pigs   49

CINDERELLA

I guess you think you know this story.
You don't. The real one's much more gory.
The phoney one, the one you know,
Was cooked up years and years ago,
And made to sound all soft and sappy
Just to keep the children happy.
Mind you, they got the first bit right,
The bit where, in the dead of night,
The Ugly Sisters, jewels and all,
Departed for the Palace Ball,
While darling little Cinderella
Was locked up in a slimy cellar,
Where rats who wanted things to eat,
Began to nibble at her feet.
She bellowed, 'Help!' and 'Let me out!'
The Magic Fairy heard her shout.
Appearing in a blaze of light,
She said, 'My dear, are you all right?'

'*All right?*' cried Cindy. 'Can't you see
'I feel as rotten as can be!'
She beat her fist against the wall,
And shouted, 'Get me to the Ball!
'There is a Disco at the Palace!
'The rest have gone and I am jalous!
'I want a dress! I want a coach!
'And earrings and a diamond brooch!
'And silver slippers, two of those!
'And lovely nylon panty-hose!
'Done up like that I'll guarantee
'The handsome Prince will fall for me!'
The Fairy said, 'Hang on a tick.'
She gave her wand a mighty flick
And quickly, in no time at all,
Cindy was at the Palace Ball!
It made the Ugly Sisters wince
To see her dancing with the Prince.
She held him very tight and pressed
Herself against his manly chest.
The Prince himself was turned to pulp,
All *he* could do was gasp and gulp.

Then midnight struck. She shouted, 'Heck!
'I've got to run to save my neck!'
The Prince cried, 'No! Alas! Alack!'
He grabbed her dress to hold her back.
As Cindy shouted, 'Let me go!'
The dress was ripped from head to toe.
She ran out in her underwear,
And lost one slipper on the stair.
The Prince was on it like a dart,
He pressed it to his pounding heart,

'The girl this slipper fits,' he cried,
'Tomorrow morn shall be my bride!
'I'll visit every house in town
'Until I've tracked the maiden down!'
Then rather carelessly, I fear,
He placed it on a crate of beer.
At once, one of the Ugly Sisters
(The one whose face was blotched with blisters)
Sneaked up and grabbed the dainty shoe,
And quickly flushed it down the loo.

Then in its place she calmly put
The slipper from her own left foot.
Ah-ha, you see, the plot grows thicker,
And Cindy's luck starts looking sicker.
Next day, the Prince went charging down
To knock on all the doors in town.

In every house, the tension grew.
Who was the owner of the shoe?
The shoe was long and very wide.
(A normal foot got lost inside.)
Also it smelled a wee bit icky.
(The owner's feet were hot and sticky.)

Thousands of eager people came
To try it on, but all in vain.
Now came the Ugly Sisters' go.
One tried it on. The Prince screamed, 'No!'
But she screamed, 'Yes! It fits! Whoopee!
'So now you've got to marry me!'
The Prince went white from ear to ear.
He muttered, 'Let me out of here.'
'Oh no you don't! You've made a vow!
'There's no way you can back out now!'
'Off with her head!' the Prince roared back.
They chopped it off with one big whack.

This pleased the Prince. He smiled and said,
'She's prettier without her head.'
Then up came Sister Number Two,
Who yelled, 'Now *I* will try the shoe!'
'Try this instead!' the Prince yelled back.
He swung his trusty sword and *smack* –
Her head went crashing to the ground.
It bounced a bit and rolled around.
In the kitchen, peeling spuds,
Cinderella heard the thuds
Of bouncing heads upon the floor,
And poked her own head round the door.
'What's all the racket?' Cindy cried.
'Mind your own bizz,' the Prince replied.
Poor Cindy's heart was torn to shreds.
My Prince! she thought. He chops off *heads*!
How could I marry anyone
Who does that sort of thing for fun?
The Prince cried, 'Who's this dirty mutt?
'Off with her nut! Off with her nut!'
Just then, all in a blaze of light,
The Magic Fairy hove in sight,

Her Magic Wand went *swoosh* and *swish*!
'Cindy!' she cried. 'Come make a wish!
'Wish anything and have no doubt
'That I will make it come about!'
Cindy answered, 'Oh kind Fairy,
'This time I shall be more wary.
'No more Princes, no more money.
'I have had my taste of honey.
'I'm wishing for a decent man.
'They're hard to find. D'you think you can?'
Within a minute, Cinderella
Was married to a lovely feller,
A simple jam-maker by trade,
Who sold good home-made marmalade.
Their house was filled with smiles and laughter
And they were happy ever after.

JACK AND THE BEANSTALK

Jack's mother said, 'We're *stony broke*!
'Go out and find some wealthy bloke
'Who'll buy our cow. Just say she's sound
'And worth at least a hundred pound.
'But don't you dare to let him know
'That she's as old as billy-o.'
Jack led the old brown cow away,
And came back later in the day,
And said, 'Oh mumsie dear, guess what
'Your clever little boy has got.
'I got, I really don't know how,
'A super trade-in for our cow.'
The mother said, 'You little creep,
'I'll bet you sold her much too cheap.'
When Jack produced one lousy bean,
His startled mother, turning green,
Leaped high up in the air and cried,
'I'm *absolutely stupefied*!

'You crazy boy! D'you really mean
'You sold our Daisy for a bean?'
She snatched the bean. She yelled,
  'You chump!'
And flung it on the rubbish-dump.
Then summoning up all her power,
She beat the boy for half an hour,
Using (and nothing could be meaner)
The handle of a vacuum-cleaner.
At ten p.m. or thereabout,
The little bean began to sprout.
By morning it had grown so tall
You couldn't see the top at all.
Young Jack cried, 'Mum, admit it now!
'It's better than a rotten cow!'
The mother said, 'You lunatic!
'Where are the beans that I can pick?
'There's not *one bean*! It's bare as bare!'
'No no!' cried Jack. 'You look up there!
'Look very high and you'll behold
'Each single leaf is solid gold!'
By gollikins, the boy was right!
Now, glistening in the morning light,

13

The mother actually perceives
A mass of lovely golden leaves!
She yells out loud, 'My sainted souls!
'I'll sell the Mini, buy a Rolls!
'Don't stand and gape, you little clot!
'Get up there quick and grab the lot!'
Jack was nimble, Jack was keen.
He scrambled up the mighty bean.
Up up he went without a stop,
But just as he was near the top,
A ghastly frightening thing occurred –
Not far above his head he heard
A big deep voice, a rumbling thing
That made the very heavens ring.
It shouted loud,

    'FE

FI

FO

FUM

'I SMELL THE BLOOD OF
  AN ENGLISHMAN!'
Jack was frightened, Jack was quick,
And down he climbed in half a tick.
'Oh mum!' he gasped. 'Believe you me
'There's something nasty up our tree!
'I saw him, mum! My gizzard froze!
'A Giant with a clever nose!'

'*A clever nose!*' his mother hissed.
'You must be going round the twist!'
'He smelled me out, I swear it, mum!
'He said he *smelled* an Englishman!'
The mother said, 'And well he might!
'I've told you every single night

'To take a bath because you smell,
'But would you do it? Would you hell!
'You even make your mother shrink
'Because of your unholy stink!'
Jack answered, 'Well, if you're so clean
'Why don't *you* climb the crazy bean.'
The mother cried, 'By gad, I will!
'There's life within the old dog still!'
She hitched her skirts above her knee
And disappeared right up the tree.
Now would the Giant smell his mum?
Jack listened for the *fee-fo-fum.*
He gazed aloft. He wondered when
The dreaded words would come . . . And then . . .
From somewhere high above the ground
There came a frightful crunching sound.
He heard the Giant mutter twice,
'By gosh, that tasted very nice.
'Although' (and this in grumpy tones)
'I wish there weren't so many bones.'
'By Christopher!' Jack cried. 'By gum!
'The Giant's eaten up my mum!

'He smelled her out! She's in his belly!
'I had a hunch that she was smelly.'
Jack stood there gazing longingly
Upon the huge and golden tree.
He murmured softly, 'Golly-gosh,
'I guess I'll *have* to take a wash
'If I am going to climb this tree
'Without the Giant smelling me.
'In fact, a bath's my only hope . . .'
He rushed indoors and grabbed the soap.
He scrubbed his body everywhere.
He even washed and rinsed his hair.
He did his teeth, he blew his nose
And went out smelling like a rose.
Once more he climbed the mighty bean.
The Giant sat there, gross, obscene,
Muttering through his vicious teeth
(While Jack sat tensely just beneath),
Muttering loud, 'FEE FI FO FUM,
'RIGHT NOW I CAN'T SMELL
   ANYONE.'

Jack waited till the Giant slept,
Then out along the boughs he crept
And gathered so much gold, I swear
He was an instant millionaire.
'A bath,' he said, 'does seem to pay.
'I'm going to have one every day.'

SNOW-WHITE AND THE SEVEN DWARFS

When little Snow-White's mother died,
The King, her father, up and cried,
'Oh, what a nuisance! What a life!
'Now I must find another wife!'
(It's never easy for a king
To find himself that sort of thing.)
He wrote to every magazine
And said, 'I'm looking for a Queen.'
At least ten thousand girls replied
And begged to be the royal bride.
The King said with a shifty smile,
'I'd like to give each one a trial.'
However, in the end he chose
A lady called Miss Maclahose,
Who brought along a curious toy
That seemed to give her endless joy –
This was a mirror framed in brass,
A MAGIC TALKING LOOKING-GLASS.

Ask it something day or night,
It always got the answer right.
For instance, if you were to say,
'Oh Mirror, what's for lunch today?'
The thing would answer in a trice,
'Today it's scrambled eggs and rice.'
Now every day, week in week out,
The spoiled and stupid Queen would shout,
'Oh Mirror Mirror on the wall,
'Who is the fairest of them all?'
The Mirror answered every time,
'Oh Madam, you're the Queen sublime.
'You are the only one to charm us,
'Queen, you are the cat's pyjamas.'
For ten whole years the silly Queen
Repeated this absurd routine.

Then suddenly, one awful day,
She heard the Magic Mirror say,
'From now on, Queen, you're *Number Two*.
'*Snow-White* is prettier than you!'
The Queen went absolutely wild.
She yelled, 'I'm going to scrag that child!
'I'll cook her flaming goose! I'll skin 'er!
'I'll have her rotten guts for dinner!'
She called the Huntsman to her study.
She shouted at him, 'Listen, buddy!
'You drag that filthy girl outside,
'And see you take her for a ride!
'Thereafter slit her ribs apart
'And bring me back her bleeding heart!'
The Huntsman dragged the lovely child
Deep deep into the forest wild.
Fearing the worst, poor Snow-White spake.
She cried, 'Oh please give me a break!'
The knife was poised, the arm was strong,
She cried again, 'I've done no *wrong*!'
The Huntsman's heart began to flutter.
It melted like a pound of butter.

He murmured, 'Okay, beat it, kid,'
And you can bet your life she did.
Later, the Huntsman made a stop
Within the local butcher's shop,
And there he bought, for safety's sake,
A bullock's heart and one nice steak.
'Oh Majesty! Oh Queen!' he cried,
'That rotten little girl has died!
'And just to prove I didn't cheat,
'I've brought along these bits of meat.'

The Queen cried out, 'Bravissimo!
'I trust you killed her nice and slow.'
Then (this is the disgusting part)
The Queen sat down and ate the heart!
(I only hope she cooked it well.
Boiled heart can be as tough as hell.)
While all of this was going on,
Oh where, oh where had Snow-White gone?

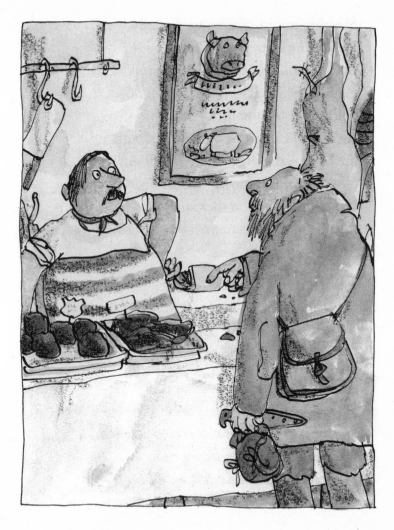

She'd found it easy, being pretty,
To hitch a ride in to the city,
And there she'd got a job, unpaid,
As general cook and parlour-maid
With seven funny little men,
Each one not more than three foot ten,
Ex horse-race jockeys, all of them.
These Seven Dwarfs, though awfully nice,
Were guilty of one shocking vice –
They squandered all of their resources
At the race-track backing horses.
(When they hadn't backed a winner,
None of them got any dinner.)
One evening, Snow-White said, 'Look here,
'I think I've got a great idea.
'Just leave it all to me, okay?
'And no more gambling till I say.'
That very night, at eventide,
Young Snow-White hitched another ride,
And then, when it was very late,
She slipped in through the Palace gate.
The King was in his counting house

Counting out his money,
The Queen was in the parlour
Eating bread and honey,
The footmen and servants slept
So no one saw her as she crept

On tip-toe through the mighty hall
And grabbed THE MIRROR off the wall.
As soon as she had got it home,
She told the Senior Dwarf (or Gnome)
To ask it what he wished to know.
'Go on!' she shouted. 'Have a go!'
He said, 'Oh Mirror, please don't joke!
'Each one of us is stony broke!
'Which horse will win tomorrow's race,
'The Ascot Gold Cup Steeplechase?'
The Mirror whispered sweet and low,
'The horse's name is Mistletoe.'

The Dwarfs went absolutely daft,
They kissed young Snow-White fore and aft,
Then rushed away to raise some dough
With which to back old Mistletoe.
They pawned their watches, sold the car,
They borrowed money near and far.
(For much of it they had to thank
The manager of Barclays Bank.)
They went to Ascot and of course
For once they backed the winning horse.
Thereafter, every single day,
The Mirror made the bookies pay.
Each Dwarf and Snow-White got a share,
And each was soon a millionaire,
Which shows that gambling's not a sin
Provided that you always win.

GOLDILOCKS AND THE THREE BEARS

This famous wicked little tale
Should never have been put on sale.
It is a mystery to me
Why loving parents cannot see
That this is actually a book
About a brazen little crook.
Had I the chance I wouldn't fail
To clap young Goldilocks in jail.
Now just imagine how *you'd* feel
If you had cooked a lovely meal,
Delicious porridge, steaming hot,
Fresh coffee in the coffee-pot,
With maybe toast and marmalade,
The table beautifully laid,
One place for you and one for dad,
Another for your little lad.
Then dad cries, 'Golly-gosh! Gee-whizz!
'Oh cripes! How hot this porridge is!

'Let's take a walk along the street
'Until it's cool enough to eat.'
He adds, 'An early morning stroll
'Is good for people on the whole.
'It makes your appetite improve
'It also helps your bowels to move.'
No proper wife would dare to question
Such a sensible suggestion,
Above all not at breakfast-time
When men are seldom at their prime.
No sooner are you down the road
Than Goldilocks, that little toad,
That nosey thieving little louse,
Comes sneaking in your empty house.
She looks around. She quickly notes
Three bowls brimful of porridge oats.
And while still standing on her feet,
She grabs a spoon and starts to eat.
I say again, how *would* you feel
If you had made this lovely meal
And some delinquent little tot
Broke in and gobbled up the lot?

But wait! That's not the worst of it!
Now comes the most distressing bit.
You are of course a houseproud wife,
And all your happy married life
You have collected lovely things
Like gilded cherubs wearing wings,
And furniture by Chippendale
Bought at some famous auction sale.
But your most special valued treasure,
The piece that gives you endless pleasure,
Is one small children's dining-chair,
Elizabethan, very rare.

It is in fact your joy and pride,
Passed down to you on grandma's side.
But Goldilocks, like many freaks,
Does not appreciate antiques.
She doesn't care, she doesn't mind,
And now she plonks her fat behind
Upon this dainty precious chair,
And crunch! It busts beyond repair.
A nice girl would at once exclaim,
'Oh dear! Oh heavens! What a shame!'
Not Goldie. She begins to swear.
She bellows, 'What a lousy chair!'
And uses *one* disgusting word
That luckily you've never heard.
(I dare not write it, even hint it.
Nobody would ever print it.)
You'd think by now this little skunk
Would have the sense to do a bunk.
But no. I very much regret
She hasn't nearly finished yet.
Deciding she would like a rest,
She says, 'Let's see which bed is best.'

Upstairs she goes and tries all three.
(Here comes the next catastrophe.)
Most educated people choose
To rid themselves of socks and shoes
Before they clamber into bed.
But Goldie didn't give a shred.
Her filthy shoes were thick with grime,
And mud and mush and slush and slime.
Worse still, upon the heel of one
Was something that a dog had done.
I say once more, what *would* you think
If all this horrid dirt and stink
Was smeared upon your eiderdown
By this revolting little clown?
(The famous story has no clues
To show the girl removed her shoes.)
Oh, what a tale of crime on crime!
Let's check it for a second time.

Crime One, the prosecution's case:
She breaks and enters someone's place.

Crime Two, the prosecutor notes:
She steals a bowl of porridge oats.

Crime Three: She breaks a precious chair
Belonging to the Baby Bear.

Crime Four: She smears each spotless sheet
With filthy messes from her feet.

A judge would say without a blink,
'Ten years' hard labour in the clink!'
But in the book, as you will see,
The little beast gets off scot-free,
While tiny children near and far
Shout, 'Goody-good! Hooray! Hurrah!'

'Poor darling Goldilocks!' they say,
'Thank goodness that she got away!'
Myself, I think I'd rather send
Young Goldie to a sticky end.
'Oh daddy!' cried the Baby Bear,
'My porridge gone! It isn't fair!'
'Then go upstairs,' the Big Bear said,
'Your porridge is upon the bed.
'But as it's inside mademoiselle,
'You'll have to eat *her* up as well.'

LITTLE RED RIDING HOOD
AND THE WOLF

As soon as Wolf began to feel
That he would like a decent meal,
He went and knocked on Grandma's door.
When Grandma opened it, she saw
The sharp white teeth, the horrid grin,
And Wolfie said, 'May I come in?'

Poor Grandmamma was terrified,
'He's going to eat me up!' she cried.
And she was absolutely right.
He ate her up in one big bite.
But Grandmamma was small and tough,
And Wolfie wailed, 'That's not enough!
'I haven't yet begun to feel
'That I have had a decent meal!'
He ran around the kitchen yelping,
'I've *got* to have another helping!'
Then added with a frightful leer,
'I'm therefore going to wait right here
'Till Little Miss Red Riding Hood
'Comes home from walking in the wood.'
He quickly put on Grandma's clothes.
(Of course he hadn't eaten those.)
He dressed himself in coat and hat.
He put on shoes and after that
He even brushed and curled his hair,
Then sat himself in Grandma's chair.
In came the little girl in red.
She stopped. She stared. And then she said,

'*What great big ears you have, Grandma.*'
'*All the better to hear you with,*' the Wolf replied.
'*What great big eyes you have, Grandma,*'
    said Little Red Riding Hood.
'*All the better to see you with,*' the Wolf replied.

He sat there watching her and smiled.
He thought, I'm going to eat this child.

Compared with her old Grandmamma
She's going to taste like caviare.

Then Little Red Riding Hood said,
*'But Grandma, what a lovely great big furry coat
    you have on.'*

'That's wrong!' cried Wolf. 'Have you forgot
'To tell me what BIG TEETH I've got?
'Ah well, no matter what you say,
'I'm going to eat you anyway.'
The small girl smiles. One eyelid flickers.
She whips a pistol from her knickers.
She aims it at the creature's head
And *bang bang bang*, she shoots him dead.

A few weeks later, in the wood,
I came across Miss Riding Hood.
But what a change! No cloak of red,
No silly hood upon her head.
She said, 'Hello, and do please note
'My lovely furry WOLFSKIN COAT.'

THE THREE LITTLE PIGS

The animal I really dig
Above all others is the pig.
Pigs are noble. Pigs are clever,
Pigs are courteous. However,
Now and then, to break this rule,
One meets a pig who is a fool.
What, for example, would you say
If strolling through the woods one day,
Right there in front of you you saw
A pig who'd built his house of STRAW?
The Wolf who saw it licked his lips,
And said, 'That pig has had his chips.'

'Little pig, little pig, let me come in!'
'No, no, by the hairs on my chinny-chin-chin!'
'Then I'll huff and I'll puff and I'll blow
  your house in!'

The little pig began to pray,
But Wolfie blew his house away.
He shouted, 'Bacon, pork and ham!
'Oh, what a lucky Wolf I am!'
And though he ate the pig quite fast,
He carefully kept the tail till last.
Wolf wandered on, a trifle bloated.
Surprise, surprise, for soon he noted
Another little house for pigs,
And this one had been built of TWIGS!

'Little pig, little pig, let me come in!'
'No, no, by the hairs of my chinny-chin-chin!'
'Then I'll huff and I'll puff and I'll blow
  your house in!'

The Wolf said, 'Okay, here we go!'
He then began to blow and blow.
The little pig began to squeal.
He cried, 'Oh Wolf, you've had *one* meal!
'Why can't we talk and make a deal?'
The Wolf replied, 'Not on your nelly!'
And soon the pig was in his belly.
'Two juicy little pigs!' Wolf cried,
'But still I am not satisfied!
'I know full well my tummy's bulging,
'But oh, how I adore indulging.'
So creeping quietly as a mouse,
The Wolf approached another house,
A house which also had inside
A little piggy trying to hide.
But this one, Piggy Number Three,
Was bright and brainy as could be.

No straw for him, no twigs or sticks.
This pig had built his house of BRICKS.
'You'll not get *me*!' the Piggy cried.
'I'll blow you down!' the Wolf replied.
'You'll need,' Pig said, 'a lot of puff,
'And I don't think you've got enough.'
Wolf huffed and puffed and blew and blew.
The house stayed up as good as new.
'If I can't blow it *down*,' Wolf said,
'I'll have to blow it *up* instead.
'I'll come back in the dead of night
'And blow it up with dynamite!'
Pig cried, 'You brute! I might have known!'
Then, picking up the telephone,
He dialled as quickly as he could
The number of Red Riding Hood.

'Hello,' she said. 'Who's speaking? *Who?*
'Oh, hello Piggy, how d'you do?'
Pig cried, 'I need your help, Miss Hood!
'Oh help me, please! D'you think you could?'
'I'll try, of course,' Miss Hood replied.
'What's on your mind?' . . . '*A Wolf!*' Pig cried.
'I know you've dealt with wolves before,
'And now I've got one at my door!'
'My darling Pig,' she said, 'my sweet,
'That's something *really* up my street.
'I've just begun to wash my hair.
'But when it's dry, I'll be right there.'
A short while later, through the wood,
Came striding brave Miss Riding Hood.
The Wolf stood there, his eyes ablaze
And yellowish, like mayonnaise.
His teeth were sharp, his gums were raw,
And spit was dripping from his jaw.
Once more the maiden's eyelid flickers.
She draws the pistol from her knickers.
Once more, she hits the vital spot,
And kills him with a single shot.

Pig, peeping through the window, stood
And yelled, 'Well done, Miss Riding Hood!'

Ah, Piglet, you must never trust
Young ladies from the upper crust.
For now, Miss Riding Hood, one notes,
Not only has *two* wolfskin coats,
But when she goes from place to place,
She has a PIGSKIN TRAVELLING CASE.

HAVE YOU HEARD

REVOLTING RHYMES & DIRTY BEASTS

read by MIRIAM MARGOLYES, STEPHEN MANGAN & TAMSIN GREIG?

Illustrations © Quentin Blake

YOU HAVEN'T?

Download the audiobook or get the CD!

www.roalddahl.com/apps

George Kranky has a grizzly old grunion of a Grandma, who is just as horrid as the Ugly Sisters and Snow-White's stepmother.

Read on as George comes up with a marvellous plan to teach her a lesson she won't forget . . .

GEORGE'S MARVELLOUS MEDICINE

The Marvellous Plan

George sat himself down at the table in the kitchen. He was shaking a little. Oh, how he hated Grandma! He really *hated* that horrid old witchy woman. And all of a sudden he had a tremendous urge to *do something* about her. Something *whopping*. Something *absolutely terrific*. A *real shocker*. A sort of explosion. He wanted to blow away the witchy smell that hung about her in the next room. He may have been only eight years old but he was a brave little boy. He was ready to take this old woman on.

'I'm not going to be frightened by *her*,' he said softly to himself. But he *was* frightened. And that's why he wanted suddenly to explode her away.

Well . . . not quite away. But he did want to shake the old woman up a bit.

Very well, then. What should it be, this whopping terrific exploding shocker for Grandma?

He would have liked to put a firework banger under her chair but he didn't have one.

He would have liked to put a long green snake down the back of her dress but he didn't have a long green snake.

He would have liked to put six big black rats in the room with her and lock the door but he didn't have six big black rats.

As George sat there pondering this interesting problem, his eye fell upon the bottle of Grandma's brown medicine standing on the sideboard. Rotten stuff it seemed to be. Four times a day a large spoonful of it was shovelled into her mouth and it didn't do her the slightest bit of good. She was always just as horrid after she'd had it as she'd been before. The whole point of medicine, surely, was to make a person better. If it didn't do that, then it was quite useless.

So-ho! thought George suddenly. *Ah-ha! Ho-hum!* I know exactly what I'll do. I shall make her a *new* medicine, one that is so strong and so fierce and so fantastic it will either cure her completely or blow off the top of her head. I'll make her a *magic medicine*, a medicine no doctor in the world has ever made before.

George looked at the kitchen clock. It said five past ten. There was nearly an hour left before Grandma's next dose was due at eleven.

'Here we go, then!' cried George, jumping up from the table. 'A magic medicine it shall be!'

'So give me a bug and a jumping flea,
Give me two snails and lizards three,
And a slimy squiggler from the sea,
And the poisonous sting of a bumblebee,
And the juice from the fruit of the ju-jube tree,
And the powdered bone of a wombat's knee.
And one hundred other things as well
Each with a rather nasty smell.
I'll stir them up, I'll boil them long,
A mixture tough, a mixture strong.
And then, heigh-ho, and down it goes,
A nice big spoonful (hold your nose)
Just gulp it down and have no fear.
"How do you like it, Granny dear?"

Will she go pop? Will she explode?
Will she go flying down the road?
Will she go poof in a puff of smoke?
Start fizzing like a can of Coke?
Who knows? Not I. Let's wait and see.
(I'm glad it's neither you nor me.)
Oh Grandma, if you only knew
What I have got in store for you!'

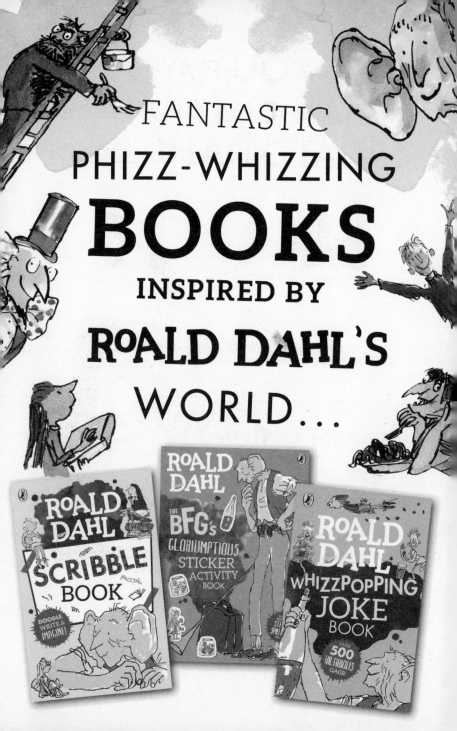

FANTASTIC
PHIZZ-WHIZZING
BOOKS
INSPIRED BY
ROALD DAHL'S
WORLD...

Have **YOU** PLAYED the **FANTASTICALLY** FUN **NEW** ROALD DAHL apps?

www.roalddahl.com/apps

How Many
Have you Read?

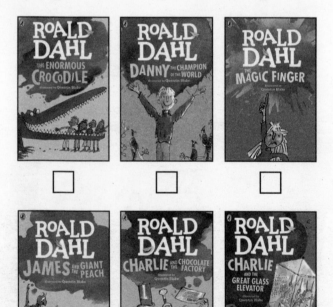

Fewer than 5?

WHOOPSY-SPLUNKERS!

You've got some reading to do!

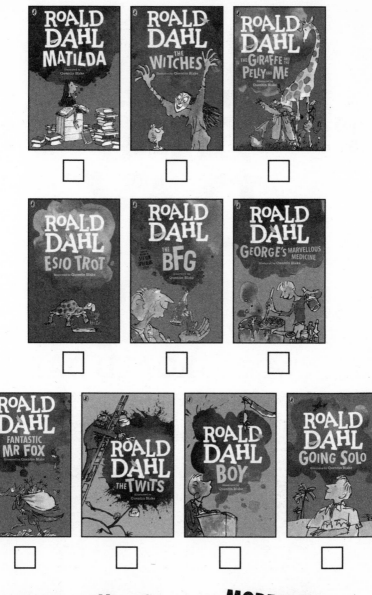

BETWEEN 5 AND 10?
Wonderful surprises await!
Keep reading . . .

MORE THAN 10?
Whoopee!
Which was your favourite?

ROALD DAHL DAY

CELEBRATE

THE PHIZZ-WHIZZING WORLD of ROALD DAHL

EVERY YEAR on 13th SEPTEMBER!

JOIN THE PARTY AT
www.roalddahl.com

STORIES ARE **GOOD** FOR **YOU.**

Roald Dahl said,
*'If you have good thoughts, they will shine
out of your face like sunbeams and you
will always look lovely.'*

We believe in doing good things.
That's why ten per cent of all Roald Dahl income*
goes to our charity partners. We have supported causes
including: specialist children's nurses, grants for
families in need, and educational outreach programmes.
Thank you for helping us to sustain this vital work.

Find out more at roalddahl.com

The Roald Dahl Charitable Trust is a registered UK charity (no. 1119330).
* All author payments and royalty income net of third-party commissions.

That's it.
The end of the book.

HERE IS
one LAST **WORD**,
invented by **Roald Dahl** HIMSELF.
Make sure you KEEP IT SAFE.

CHATBAG

Noun: Someone who talks a lot.